Many, many years ago, there lived an old man in the old city of Damascus. On his back, he carried a large chest and with it he walked from one neighborhood to the next. Whenever he passed through our alley, he would call out with a singing voice: "Come children; come and listen to my stories. It costs nothing to listen. And for only one piaster, you will be able to see the wonders of the world and brave Sami riding on a lion. All for only one piaster!"

The old man did not come to our neighborhood often—maybe once a month. The moment I heard his voice, I would run to my mother and ask her for some money. We never knew when he was likely to show up again. Sometimes he would come minutes after I had just spent the last of my money on ice cream. It was, of course, not possible to ask Mother for money twice in the same day. But even those without any money would run out to the street to meet him. And before the old man could reach the middle of the alley, he would be surrounded by children jumping with excitement, with some waving their coins, hoping to be seated first.

The old man would then set his huge wonder chest down and place in front of it the little bench that he carried over his shoulder. The bench was just big enough to seat four children, and it was placed close enough so that all four could look through its small peepholes.

The old man never began to tell his stories right away. First, he would look at us curiously. He would then ask about our fathers' professions, and he would always ask for a glass of water. Whoever brought him some water would be allowed to watch the show for free. So whenever there was nothing except holes in my pocket and I heard the storyteller's voice, I would rush to fill up a jug with fresh water and run to bring it to him. Often, though, I wasn't the only one to bring the old man water and this caused some arguments among us. Watching us quarrel, the old man chuckled happily and allowed the first four water carriers to look through the peepholes for free.

We had to get very close to the chest until our noses touched the peepholes. This was the only way we could see the pictures inside the wonder chest. The sliver of light that came in through the openings in the top of the chest was just enough to allow us to see the pictures clearly.

Then the old man started telling his story. At the same time, he moved two wands with his shaking hands. Suddenly, colorful pictures would appear before our eyes and start to move from left to right.

The wonderful old drawings shimmered with mystery in the dim light. Was it the special light or the storyteller's magical voice that made it look as if living creatures were leaping out of the picture roll? The figures rode horses; they had fights with each other; and they even kissed in front of our eyes.

As the old man told his stories, he would often change his voice. Sometimes it was loud; sometimes it was gentle. Sometimes it was old; sometimes it was young. And he also sang songs from old times. I can still see it as if it were taking place now in front of me: neighbors, merchants, and street sweepers would stop in the middle of the street or in front of their houses to listen to the storyteller's wonderful voice. Often, you'd see people secretly wipe tears from their eyes when, in the story, a blind person or prisoner would lament about his fate or cry about his misfortune.

The storyteller of Damascus always told the same old stories, which all of us already knew by heart. But each time he told a story, he would tell it differently and it felt as if you were hearing it for the first time.

The storyteller began his first story...

Once upon a time, there lived a shepherd boy named Sami. He was, as you all can see, more beautiful than the moon and braver than a panther. But, he was poor as a beggar. One day, as he was leading his master's flock of sheep and goats to the village spring, his eyes set on the young Leyla. She was more beautiful than a rose and more graceful than a gazelle. Wonderstruck, Sami stopped. And stared. Suddenly, Leyla turned around and asked him, in her gentle voice, if he wouldn't mind helping her lift the heavy water jug on to her shoulder.

In the name of Allah, my little ones, let me tell you that Leyla could have easily lifted the jar all by herself, but she'd had her eyes on Sami for some time and really wanted to speak with him.

Sami lifted the jar. But as he was about to place it gently on Leyla's shoulder, he slipped and his lips brushed against her left cheek. I am not sure... I don't know if he did it on purpose or not. Here, in this picture, you can see that wonderful kiss.

From this spring day on, Leyla and Sami would meet every evening, at the same place. Soon, the entire village was talking only about their love.

But Leyla was the daughter of the richest farmer in the village. Her father wanted her to marry an old, but very rich sheikh. You can imagine just how angry her father was when he found out about his daughter's secret meetings with the shepherd boy. He fumed with rage. Here you can see the awful man in his violent temper.

He forbade Leyla to see Sami ever again. When she did not follow his order, he locked her up in the cellar for seven days, feeding her only bread and water. He had a heart as cold as stone. Allah should punish him for what he had done! But, my beloved children, nothing could stop Leyla from seeing Sami in secret again. And so, for these young lovers, time passed as fast as a waterfall.

Fall arrived and the farmers were happy with their bountiful harvest. But their happiness was short-lived, for one day a gang of robbers invaded the village. They plundered houses and barns. Can you see their scary mustaches and their shining swords?

When the leader of the gang saw Leyla, he grabbed her and lifted her onto his horse, then fled. Here you can see Leyla calling for help. Leyla's father cried loudly and pulled his hair: "Help! My daughter! My only pride! Have pity on me! Please help me to save her!" But not one villager wanted to get involved.

On that day, Sami had taken his flock to a faraway pasture. When he returned home in the evening, he learned about what happened and vowed never to rest until Leyla was freed. Leyla's father, the villain, faithfully agreed to Leyla and Sami's marriage and promised Sami a magnificent wedding if he were to rescue his daughter.

Sami got on the white horse that Leyla's father had allowed him to borrow and went looking for the robbers. What a beautiful horse! Can you see, my children? I would even give up my wonder chest for it. I could spend days praising this precious horse, but I know you would like me to go on with the story…

Sami followed the robbers for three days and three nights. At the crack of dawn on the fourth day, Sami caught up with them. When Leyla saw him, she wriggled out of the ropes of her captors and ran to him. Sami fended off the robbers with his left hand, and with his right one he helped her onto the back of the magnificent white horse. Here you can see Sami and Leyla returning to the village. Everyone was overjoyed and Sami was welcomed back as a hero. Can you see the villagers dancing happily? The big man with the red rose in his hand is the village singer. He sang a song about the two lovers. And that man with the long face—yes, there at the top right-hand corner of the picture—is Leyla's father. The people celebrated for three days and three nights.

And the more people shared their happiness, the more joyous the festivities became.

When Sami reminded Leyla's father of his promise, her father pretended to be dangerously ill. He said with a weak voice: "Only the milk of a lioness can cure me. Bring me the milk and I will allow the marriage to take place." He was so mean! And this time he would not lend Sami the white horse because a lion might eat it.

Sami got on his little donkey and left. Leyla's father was now sure that the shepherd boy would never return. Everybody knew how dangerous it was to get milk from a lioness. Sami arrived at the gorge where many lions lived. He got off his donkey, tied it to a tree, and walked up to the first lioness and said: "Please, excuse me. I am in love and need some of your milk." The lioness understood his grief and allowed Sami to milk her. He was touched by the lioness's kindheartedness. Can you see how the lioness licked Sami's face as he milked her? A second lioness also had a soft spot in her heart for lovers. She too let Sami milk her. But when the male lions saw what Sami was doing, they tried to attack him. He scared them away with his left hand while milking with his right one. Again and again, he had to shoo the lions away, so it took a while to fill the jar with the prized milk. When Sami went to fetch his donkey, he discovered that it had been eaten by the lions. Sami became angry. He grabbed the most powerful lion's ears and shouted: "Because you killed my donkey, you now have to take me home!"

Sami got on the lion's back and rode to the village with the jar of milk in his hand. Here you can see Sami on the lion. Look how the people, the chickens, and the donkeys steered away when they saw Sami riding to the village square on a lion. Meanwhile, Leyla's father turned white when he saw Sami and the lion at his doorstep.

"Get better soon," Sami said as he handed over the milk to the trembling father. He then turned to the lion and said, "Never eat the donkey of a man in love again," and set him free to go back to his family.

As you can see, Leyla's father recovered quickly from his shock and said: "You are the bravest in the village, but also the poorest. I will give you my daughter, but only after you bring me three hundred camels as dowry." He made it sound so easy. But how could Sami acquire three hundred camels, knowing that a single camel would cost a fortune? Sami did not even own a goat.

The father knew all too well that Sami could never buy three hundred camels.

Leyla did not want to marry the old sheikh or any of the three princes. She only wanted Sami. Sami was overcome with sadness and could not sleep. He took on whatever job was offered to him and saved each single piaster. He traded in cheese, milk, and sheepskins but only earned a little money. After two years, he was completely worn out and had barely saved enough money to buy one camel. "What should I do?" he asked a wise old neighbor. The wise man answered: "Work alone would not help. You have to find another solution. The sultan owns three thousand camels. It wouldn't be a huge loss for him if you were to take three hundred camels from his herd. Go to Damascus and try your luck."

Filled with hope, Sami made his way to Damascus. Here you can see how beautiful the city looked at that time. You can see the gardens, the narrow alleyways and the Grand Mosque. And this here is the sultan's herd of camels. Can you see how massive it is? It would be impossible to count the number of camels in the herd. When Sami asked one of the herders if he could take three hundred camels, the herder laughed, thinking it was a joke. It made him laugh so hard the herder replied: "Why three hundred only? Take five hundred!"

"No thanks, three hundred is enough," answered Sami politely. The herder was astonished when he saw Sami counting the camels. Several other herders rushed to the scene to chase Sami away. But Sami would not let anything stand in his way. He pushed each herder to the ground with his left hand and with his right hand he continued to count until he reached three hundred. But when he tried to leave with the camels, he was totally surrounded by soldiers who captured him and brought him before a judge.

The judge looked at Sami from his high stool and asked in a scornful voice: "Why did you try to steal three hundred camels and beat the herders?"

"Because I am in love," answered Sami calmly.

"You are in love? Are you mad? Did I hear you say 'in love'? For many years, I have listened to stories and fairy tales from thieves and swindlers, but I have never heard this one before. You stole three hundred camels from His Majesty. Almighty Allah, he stole because he is in love! Take this thief away. He'll get five years for what he has done," shouted the judge.

It was Sami's third day in prison. He thought of Leyla day and night and his longing to see her grew stronger and stronger. He passed the time by prying out little pieces of stone from the wall and throwing them at the guards in the prison yard. Sami, like all young shepherds, could hit things a great distance away with his slingshot. One day, Sami discovered a white dove on the roof facing his prison cell window. She looked sad and Sami asked her about her grief.

The dove groaned: "You too would be sad, if you suffered my misfortune. I am not a dove; I am a woman. Someone put a spell on me..."

"But this is a long story, which I shall tell you later. As if my life weren't hard enough, a vulture has been following me around all morning and has tried to eat me. I told the vulture that I am not a dove, but a woman! And what does this terrible beast say in reply? 'Either way, you will be delicious!' He tries to ambush me everywhere: behind every shadow and in every cloud. I feel utterly miserable!"

The dove wept and Sami tried to comfort her. Suddenly, he noticed a black dot in the sky. It came closer and closer and got bigger and bigger. He instantly recognized the vulture and quickly pried a little stone out of the wall and placed it in his slingshot. The moment the beast got close to the dove and was about to grab her with his claws, a stone hit him in his chest. The vulture screamed and flew away. The dove breathed a sigh of relief and flew to Sami. Here you can see how Sami tenderly strokes her head and tells her his own story.

"You have saved my life. For this you can make one wish," said the dove. Sami smiled: "How can you help me? I need three hundred camels, not three hundred eggs."

"You shall have your camels. I once saved the life of the Crown Prince. In return, he fulfills all my wishes," said the dove and flew away.

The sultan had an only son, whom the dove had saved from the bite of a deadly snake. But, children, this is a long story, which I promise to tell you at another time. The prince loved the dove. So when she flew into his room and asked him to follow her, he hurried behind her without a question.

Here you can see him on the castle's staircase. To his surprise, the dove led him all the way to the prison gate. The prince ordered the guards to open the gate. He rushed into the cell where Sami was being held and listened to the shepherd boy's touching story. Here you can see how the prince listened attentively.

Then the prince hurried to his father, the sultan, and asked him to help the shepherd who was in love. And so it was that the sultan granted Sami his freedom and sent him off with a gift of three hundred camels.

Sami rode back to the village as quickly as he could. Here you can see how the people cheered on his arrival. Although the greedy father was not at all pleased, he promised that the wedding would take place during the next full moon.

Leyla and Sami had to wait for ten more days. But during the first night, the father visited a sorcerer. He gave him lots of gold to transform his daughter into a lizard. Look here, see how the sorcerer sits in front of his incense bowl as he calls the Lizard Demon. It did not take long for the demon to appear. Doesn't he look scary?

"I am your servant," said the demon. "Command and I shall obey."

"Go to Leyla, turn her into a little lizard and bring her to me," commanded the sorcerer.

There, see how the demon—like fog—slips through the cracks of the door of the room.

A short while later, the demon returned. He was furious. See how he beats up the sorcerer. The demon shouted, "Take this for making trouble for me!" and hit him again and again until the sorcerer managed to say the magic words that made the demon disappear. The sorcerer could not figure out what made the demon so angry.

Leyla woke up in a very happy mood and called out loudly: "There are only nine days left!"

On the second night, the sorcerer tried again. This time, he called for the Frog Demon. But again, after a short while, the demon returned angry and beat him up. The sorcerer had no clue why he did this. Meanwhile, Leyla slept soundly, unlike the days and weeks before. You can see how she smiles in her sleep.

The days went by and every night the sorcerer—who already had more bruises than he could count—would receive a beating from a demon. On the night before the wedding, the sorcerer called the Wasp Demon. But this time, before he let him go, he asked him what it was that made the demons so angry. "It is the smell of the most disgusting plant of all. It gives demons a stomachache which lasts for ten years," answered the demon.

"Which plant is that?" asked the sorcerer.

"You are the expert," the Wasp Demon replied. "You should know that. Woe is me! If I mention the plant's name I would suffer from a stomachache for the next fifty years. Well, Master, would you still like me to turn Leyla into a little wasp and bring her here? Or would you like me to disappear? I am in a hurry."

"No, no, go and bring her to me, but as a wasp," the sorcerer commanded.

The demon rushed to Leyla. But, just as quickly he too returned and gave the sorcerer a beating.

Dawn was breaking when the sorcerer sneaked into Leyla's room as she was sleeping. Feeling weak, he sniffed all around. There he discovered the secret that he had never read about in any of his books. "Garlic," he shouted in horror. Leyla woke up and screamed when she saw the man in her room. Hearing Leyla's voice, her brothers rushed to the room. They grabbed the sorcerer and did not let him go until he confessed to them that it was their father who wanted his daughter turned into an animal.

The next day, Leyla and Sami celebrated their wedding even though the father became ill because of his anger. Here you can see the people laughing and dancing under the wonderful full moon. Leyla and Sami had a long and happy life together. May Allah make the lives of all my listeners long and happy too.

The storyteller of Damascus told stories of great adventures. But as years went by, the pictures inside his wonder chest began to fade and fade. Many could no longer be recognized. He needed to find new pictures.

One day, the old man returned to our alley. I was fortunate; I was just about to spend my money on peanuts when I heard his voice. I elbowed my way to the front and was among the first four to watch the show. The old man began to tell his story:

From this spring day on, Colgate and Sami would meet every evening, at the same place. Soon, the entire village was talking only about their love.

It did not take long before her father found out about it and he fumed with rage. Here you can see the awful father with his clenched fists. Oh, Allah should punish him! His heart was harder than the metal of his cars.

He wanted his daughter to marry a rich, old doctor. Here you can see the doctor. His hair is as white as his coat. He always has a smile on his face. See here how he smiles as he prescribes to the angry father a box of Salperin for his migraine. But no painkiller in the world would calm his

temper down ever since Colgate's announcement that she would marry no one but Sami.

One day, a gang of robbers invaded the village. They arrived in cars and airplanes and set many houses on fire. The policemen, who normally directed traffic, were powerless. When the leader of the gang saw Colgate, he kidnapped her.

Here you can see the gang leader in his jeep. Unfortunately, you can't see Colgate in the picture. She is lying and tied up on the back seat of the car. She screamed for help, but no one could hear her because of the noise from the cars and airplanes.

On that day, Sami was with his flock far away from the village. He turned on his Filix portable radio and was lucky to get good reception. As soon as he heard the news of what had happened, he rushed back home and vowed never to rest until Colgate was freed. The father, the teary-eyed villain you see here, faithfully promised that if Sami could rescue his daughter he would be allowed to marry her. Sami left at once, riding a precious, white horse that the broken-hearted father had allowed him to borrow from his stable. On the third day, Sami and his horse arrived in a small, seedy town. Look, this is the nightclub owned by the leader of the gang. Here poor Colgate was forced to serve the customers. Sami, on his horse, charged into the club. When Colgate saw him, she threw an ice-cold Coca-Cola into the face of the nightclub owner and made her escape on the white horse with Sami.

Sami returned to the village and was welcomed as a hero. Can you see the big man with the microphone? He is the village poet. Although he is poor, he is wearing a brand-new suit that the car dealer had given him as a present. The celebration lasted for three days and three nights. Here you can see the men and women dancing and drinking merrily. And the kids were happy too because they were given chocolates.

When Sami reminded Colgate's father of his promise, the nasty man pretended to be dangerously ill. He said in a weak voice that he will fulfill his promise soon after he was cured. And the only cure for his illness was Lioness Milk. He was so mean! He wouldn't even lend Sami the white horse because a lion might eat it.

Sami instead borrowed a friend's motorcycle. His friend gave him directions to the shopping mall, where he could buy the Lioness Milk. You can see Sami almost flying on his Bubuki. And see the cloud of dust the motorcycle made! Not even a herd of one hundred camels could make that much dust! When Sami asked the saleswoman about Lioness Milk, she gave him a friendly smile as you can see here. She said: "We no longer carry Lioness Milk. But I am sure that the health food store across the street not only sells Lioness Milk, but Elephant Milk as well."

Sami ran to the store and bought the milk. But when he came out of the store, he discovered that his motorcycle was stolen. He was so upset he started to cry. A clown passed by and asked him why he was so sad. When Sami told him his story, the clown felt sorry for him. "I can give you neither a donkey nor a horse; we need them for our show. But take this old lion; we have no use for him anymore. He looks dangerous, but you should not be afraid; he does not have any teeth left."

Sami got on the tame lion and rode back to the village.

From here on the pictures were still in a good shape so the storyteller continued the story as in the past. But as years went by, more and more pictures disappeared. As the old man replaced them with ads from magazines, his story became weirder and weirder, more and more unbelievable. At one point, Sami was turned into an apprentice working at a car repair shop. And Colgate's father asked for a limousine with a sun roof instead of camels.

The children slowly began to lose interest. We were no longer eager to listen to the old man's stories anymore. We laughed and sang the songs from toothpaste and dishwashing detergent commercials as soon as he mentioned the name of one of his heroes. And sometimes, the old man felt hurt and embarrassed. He would stop in the middle of the story, lift the chest and bench onto his back, and walk away mumbling to himself.

Two years had gone by without seeing the storyteller of Damascus. Some people said that he had died. Others wondered whether he had gone mad. I had almost forgotten about him, when, all of a sudden, I heard his call. I ran outside. And there he was in the flesh. His hair was grayer than before, but his voice was as loud and cheerful as ever: "Come children; come and listen to my stories. It costs nothing to listen. And for only one piaster, you will be able to see the wonders of the world and brave Sami riding on a lion. All for only one piaster!" When the children heard his call, we all realized how much we had missed him and how excited we were to hear his stories again.

We all stood in amazement, since his wonder chest no longer had wands or picture rolls anymore. The old man sang and told stories about robbers, lions, and lovers. And the children—as before—were mesmerized and spellbound. They had big smiles and their faces beamed as they got up from the little bench. Those waiting for their turn asked: "What did you see? What can one see?"

"Awesome! It is magic!" they whispered.

I was so excited when my turn came. It was truly magical. The chest was dark. I waited patiently. Then I heard the old man's voice; it was as warm and as beautiful as ever. And he began to tell his story: "Once upon a time, there lived a shepherd boy named Sami..."

Suddenly, I saw a boy who was more beautiful than the moon and braver than a panther. But he was poor as a beggar...